GOD'S REJECT

KING PEN GEMINI
Bridget Ray, Billy Ray

Iconic Creations Entertainment

GOD'S REJECT

Dedication

This book is dedicated to my family, and my neighborhood, East 105th Street. Without you all, this book series wouldn't exist. Thank you all for being my muse, my inspiration, and my support. Between my family and the people in my community, I have been able to not only dream about this moment of publishing my first book but turn my dream into a reality.

CONTENTS

CHAPTER 1

God Said Let There Be....
You Know The Rest

God had given me all this power and these damn abilities. Why not use them for my benefit and reasoning. I know, I know, I know, this is what got me kicked out of heaven in the first place. But hey, you can't give an angel this much power and authority over weak-minded human beings on earth and all of these angels and give him limitations. What kind of shit is that? Well, I will tell you what kind of shit that is, bullshit. You wanna know why? Well, I can give you all an answer for that as well. It is because I was God's first. Yeah, I said it, his first. I was his first-born child, his first servant, the first one to love him, the first one to worship him, his first archangel, and mostly why the earth is what it is today.

I told him not to abandon the earth but to "Fill the earth with life, create others in your image as you've done with me, only without the power that I possess. Give them other life forms to tend to that are not in our image. This will make our jobs much easier as far as tending to this earth you have created." God did exactly that, and he put me in control of everything and everyone he had put on earth so I could manage his creations. Life on earth started in the Garden of Eden with Adam and Eve. God gave me a job to watch over these two life forms, guide them, and make sure they followed his every command. "Teach them, for they know nothing yet," God said. So I taught them to tend to the garden and many other things such as speech, the meaning of authority, God's laws, and all of that other junk. As time passed, Adam and Eve did not need me. I taught them everything they needed to know. So my job was done, temporarily as far as this part of the earth.

When I told God that the first two humans were ready to be on their own, God came down to the garden, took his index figure, and pointed it to an arid area of the garden. A bright light came from his finger, blinding us all. When the light went away, we witnessed something more perfect looking than God and I put together. He took a dry and deserted part of the garden area and put a beautiful fruit tree right in the center. I can remember it like it was yesterday. The grass was so soft and beautiful. The tree had giant beautiful apples hanging from the limbs and vines. These apples were pure gold, and they lit up the entire garden.

As soon as Adam and Eve laid eyes on this beautiful tree, they walked toward it to remove an apple to eat it. With a strong deep voice, God yelled, "DO NOT LAY A FINGER ON THAT TREE. For it is the TREE OF LIFE! This tree will determine the future of this earth. If this fruit remains untouched, life, peace, and goodness will forever be upon you and every other creation here on earth. If it is touched, then all life is limited. You will tend to this tree as you've done with the rest of the garden. This entire garden is yours, but this tree belongs to me."

For many years Adam and Eve followed all of God's laws, which is all they did. They were living and not existing in this world, and they never had any fun. They weren't enjoying life and all the pleasures that it offers. They were servants, that was it, nothing more. Periodically I checked up on them and created games and festivities, for they were the only ones in the Garden of Eden but not on the earth by this time due to God and myself creating other human life forms on earth (life forms in general). Even though Adam and Eve had the knowledge God and I passed down to them, they still knew nothing of themselves, well, at least Adam didn't. Adam was a strong, tall, handsome warrior, he was the perfect man, and Eve knew it. Her sexual desires came naturally and very quickly for her. Eve was an ebony goddess with beautiful long thick hair. She had full breasts, a tight stomach, round derriere, beautiful matching legs, and thighs. Her facial features were incomparable to any other woman ever to exist. She was the perfect woman all around the board, and she knew it. Adam only knew what God and I taught him. He tended to the garden with no sexual desires at all. He saw himself as only a servant to God.

On many occasions, Eve tried to seduce Adam, and every time Adam rejected her. I watched all of this happen, and while I was up in heaven surrounded by so many beautiful female angels, they were nowhere near as beautiful as this woman God created on earth. I suggested to God that we tell Adam his real purpose on earth because Adam was all brawn and had no brains. God refused and told me, "Let him learn on his own as Eve did, for they will be the first of humanity to experience sexual pleasure and reproduce more than fruit on the land without it being dictated to them."

More time went by, and Adam still had no idea what to do with Eve. Eve grew sick of Adam, for he would not touch her, and I grew tired of walking the earth with no companion and with no one to love except for God. I loved my Lord, but I'd created entire civilizations outside of Eden by now. And by now, I mean many, many, many years after the completion of the first two humans. There were hundreds of thousands, if not millions of human mortals out there, reproducing and making the earth fruitful with human life. While dumb ass Adam was the only man on earth that didn't know what the full purpose of his dick was for except to piss.

Anyway, I preached and spread the word and knowledge of God and made the earth and the humans on it his perfect worshippers. And what did I get, who did I get? At least Adam had Eve; every human had a companion. Hell, every angel had someone to love, except for me. While all of the angels were in heaven reproducing, making God's army bigger, I walked the earth and was told not to have sexual encounters with any earth human or the other angels because I was their co-creators.

I was beginning to feel that God wanted me to be alone so that I could forever be his number one angel and do his bidding. But I didn't want that. I was in love with Eve. I wanted her all to myself. I knew the only way to get Eve for myself was to get Adam out of the picture. Without Adam, I would be the next best thing for Eve, and God would permit me to be with Eve. At least, that's what I thought at the time. So I came up with a plan where I felt God would kill Adam. I figured Adam had to eat from that stupid ass tree where life literally depended on humanity's fate, but Eve had to influence him to do it. With this plan I had laid out, I made my way back to the Garden of Eden after a long journey throughout the earth, being God's slave, making the humans worship him. When I arrived at the garden, Eve stopped and stared at me lustfully. She ran up to me and hugged me, pressing her naked body against mine. At that very moment, I knew she would do anything I wanted her to do when I had sex with her. Now that she had developed sexual desire and passion, she lusted after me, and it was obvious, and I was fucking loving it.

On the other hand, Adam's dumb ass thought that I was there to deliver a message from God as usual. When Adam discovered that I wasn't, he went to gather fruit further out in the garden away from the Tree of Life. While Adam was gathering fruit from the other sections of the garden, I got the chance to catch up with Eve and tell her about the other humans on earth. Then I expressed my feelings to her, laid her under the Tree of Life, and made passionate love. I opened her up physically, mentally, and emotionally. When we were done making love, I gave her instructions. I told her to make love to Adam that night when I left the garden and convince him to eat from the Tree of Life. She said no words. She just looked at me and nodded her head yes, and kissed me.

I then got up and found Adam far out in the garden. I told Adam that he has to lay with Eve to reproduce a child in God's image. I disobeyed God and told Adam that his sole purpose on earth was to reproduce life. When I walked away from Adam, I turned into a serpent and stayed in the garden instead of leaving. I had to see my plan all the way through. Afterward, Adam found Eve and laid with her as he was instructed. He enjoyed exploring her body so much; it drove him insane. All of God's teachings went out the window. He worshiped no one but Eve at that moment. It was going just as I planned. As they laid up under the Tree of Life, I remained in the form of a serpent and hung from the Tree of Life. Eve looked at Adam and smiled because she was still thinking of the sex we just had moments before her and Adam. Then Eve looked up in the tree at me because she could still feel my presence in the garden and cracked an evil grin while I watched him penetrate her.

Eve told Adam, "If you eat from the Tree of Life, then I shall give you the son that God meant for us to create." So Adam removed the golden apple from the tree and took a bite out of it. Eve gave me another evil smile and grin when Adam ate from the tree, and I left the garden. Shortly after I had left the garden, the stars that lit the sky disappeared. It began to thunder, and lightning struck the Tree of Life, setting it on fire. The fire spread throughout the entire garden, burning and killing everything but Adam and Eve.

Later it began to rain, putting out this terrible fire. God left nothing in their garden. They had no food, their water had eventually dried up, and all of their animals had died. God was so angry; he let them go without food or water for a week. He later came down from heaven and told me to join him. When we arrived at the Garden of Eden, God asked who had disobeyed his command and looked directly at Adam. Adam would not look God in the face.

God said, "FOR THIS, THERE IS A CONSEQUENCE, FOR YOU HAVE DISOBEYED ME WHEN I TOLD YOU NOT TO EAT FROM THIS TREE. I GAVE YOU EVERYTHING IN THIS GARDEN, AND I ONLY ASKED YOU TO DO ONE THING. HOW COULD YOU DO THIS WHEN YOU KNOW THE FATE OF HUMANITY WAS LYING IN YOUR HANDS??????!!!!!! NOW YOU BOTH SHALL PERISH!!!!"

God raised his hand at Adam and Eve. He was getting ready to smite them with a thunderbolt until he looked at Eve closely. He could not help but notice that something was different about her. Now don't get me wrong, Eve was the most beautiful woman God created, but she was even more beautiful on this particular day. It was almost like she was glowing. Her presence alone lit up the garden, even though God had destroyed everything.

God then laid his hand on Eve's belly, and he smiled. He could not believe what was happening. Eve was with child. God was so happy he cried tears of joy because of it. New life was God's purpose in creating Adam and Eve, and it lifted the anger out of God and filled his heart with forgiveness. God's original plan was to end Adam and Eve's life for eating from the tree. But he did not want to take an innocent life that hadn't been born yet. Even though they disobeyed him, they served their purpose on earth, and that was to reproduce. I was never so relieved that he didn't kill Eve, but I couldn't show it.

God then told them that there was still a limit to life because of their disobedience. Yet he promised that they would live a full life. He then restored the garden and made it just as beautiful as he did the first time. I stood right beside my Lord, knowing that I had sex with the first woman on earth within a few moments before Adam. I knew that I would be the father to Eve's firstborn son, and so did she. I thought that God did not know at that time, but he did. He never mentioned a word about Eve and me, so I assumed he didn't know. But the relationship had changed between my father and me. I began to notice that he kept me really close to him as if he didn't trust me. My trips down on earth were limited, and he told me that I could not go near the Garden of Eden for a long time.

By the time I was allowed to go back to the Garden of Eden, my son was all grown up. Eve named him Cain. He looked almost exactly like me. He was tall, muscular with long silky hair, and black as night. She had also given birth to another child who was also grown up. His name was Abel, and he was the son of Adam. He was identical to his father, tall, brown-skinned with dark green eyes, and long straight hair. Eve loved both of her sons equally. She never showed a difference between the two children, but Adam did A LOT. It was so obvious that he loved Abel more than he loved Cain. Cain worked very hard to please the only man he knew as his father, but his work and good deeds would go unrecognized every damn time. Abel got all of the praise in the world from his father, even though he was not as much of a hard worker as his brother.

As I looked at how things were going in the garden, I began to become angry because I thought that God would only punish Adam for eating from the Tree of Life and that I would have Eve for myself once and for all. Instead, I had to keep my son a secret and watch a man that I truly despised be with the woman that I loved and mistreat my child. One day I had to report to God about Adam and Eve, and I recommended that God recognize Cain for his good deeds and hard work. God looked at me strangely for a moment and told me that he would visit the garden to check on the boys himself and see who deserves recognition. When he arrived at the garden, Cain bowed before God. Cain said to God, "I am blessed to be in thy presents, oh Lord. For you are the King." God walked past my son like cow shit tainting the garden, and he approached Abel. God put his hand on Abel's forehead and blessed him.

God told Abel, "Son of Adam, may you be blessed and inherit the garden as your own, for you tend to it well." God not once acknowledged my son, for he was the one to tend to the garden well. As time went by, it became evident that God showed Abel more love than he did Cain. Cain began to grow jealous of his brother. It had gotten to a point where he hated his brother and the man he called father. He even began to hate God. One day Cain was so upset and hurt, that he took Abel far away from the central part of the garden and killed his brother by strangling him with his bare hands.

When Cain returned to the central part of the garden, Adam and Eve questioned him about Abel's whereabouts because Abel was nowhere to be found in the central part of the garden. Cain said nothing. So Adam went out to look for Abel in other sections of the garden. He searched for him the whole night. The next morning Adam returned to the central part of the garden. He walked to the spot where the Tree of Life once was sitting, carrying Abel's lifeless body. He stood there in that very spot, and he screamed, with tears flowing from his eyes. Eve gently stroked her son's face while Adam held him. On the other hand,

Cain was sitting in the flower bed staring at his brother's lifeless body and cracked a smile.

I must admit, I was kind of happy myself. I got sick of them praising that little bastard. He might as well have been a God the way they worshipped that bitch. Eve screamed so loudly that she woke every angel in heaven. She cursed God, asking why he'd forsaken them. God then called upon me and said that I had to go to the Garden of Eden with him. When we arrived, Eve looked at God and asked, "WHY?!"

God looked at her with such anger and said, "ASK YOURSELF WHY. YOU DID THIS TO YOUR SON. THE MINUTE YOU LAID WITH ANOTHER MAN, THE MINUTE YOU CONVINCED ADAM TO EAT FROM THE TREE, YOU SEALED YOUR FATE, AND YOU SEALED YOUR SON ABEL'S AS WELL." God then looked at me and wrapped his hand around my neck, choking the shit out of me. Then he looked at my son with so much anger and hatred. He then told me that my son was nothing but an abomination and a child that should have never been born in the first place. He then let me drop me to the ground, gasping for air. I had never seen him so angry in my life. "FOR EVERY BROKEN LAW, IS A CONSEQUENCE," God said to Eve and me. God then walked over to my son, Cain, and said,

> "DO YOU NOT KNOW WHO YOU ARE? WHAT YOU ARE? YOU ARE WHAT YOUR FATHER IS, AND YOUR FATHER IS NOT ADAM!!!!"

> "Father, God, if Adam is not my father, then who is," said Cain."

> "You are looking at him. He stands right beside me as he gasps for air," said God angrily as he turned his head to look in my direction.

Eve and I got down on our knees, praying to God and begging him to spare our child's life. Eve continued to blame Cain's actions on Adam because of how badly he treated Cain. God responded, "WHY SHOULD I SPARE YOUR SON'S LIFE WHEN HE TOOK A LIFE?!"

God lifted his hand to smite my child and kill him, but he did not go through with it. Instead, all of his anger disappeared. He looked down at Cain and smiled and laughed. He called on some of the other angels to bury Abel. While the angels followed his command, he looked at my son again.

God then said, "YOU WILL NOT ONLY PAY FOR YOUR SINS BUT FOR YOUR PARENTS SIN AS WELL. THEREFORE I BANISH YOU TO WEST EDEN, WHERE THERE IS NO LIFE. WHERE THE NIGHT IS LONG AND THE DAYS ARE SHORT. YOU WILL TEND TO THIS LAND AS YOU'VE DONE HERE. YOU ARE NOT TO EVER RETURN TO THE GARDEN OF EDEN, NOR ARE YOU EVER TO SEE YOUR MOTHER AND FATHER AGAIN. LAST BUT NOT LEAST YOU ARE NEVER TO CALL UPON ME AGAIN FOR YOU ARE NOT WORTHY EVEN TO SPEAK MY NAME."

God then walked over to Eve and placed a curse upon her. This curse prevented her from having any more children. He then took me back to heaven, and he told me when I thought he wasn't watching me, he was. He told me that he was always watching me because I was his number one. He continued to tell me my punishments. One of my punishments was that I was banned from the Garden of Eden and could have no contact with my son nor Eve, but I still kept my position as the archangel.

Here I thought that Adam eating from the Tree of Life would reward me with a woman and a child when in the end my actions reversed on me. I thought that tree would be of no concern to me. I will admit that that was pretty damn stupid of me. As more years went by, nothing changed. Eve still could not have children, and my son was still in West Eden, where he suffered.

God did not lie when he told Cain there was no life in West Eden. It was nothing but a desert land, where it never rained and there was very little sunlight. There were no animals, no nothing. He only survived by eating the desert sands and drinking his blood from his wrist. Nothing could grow in West Eden. If Cain even tried to produce something, it would instantly die.

Eventually, my son gave up trying to live. He grew tired of eating the desert sands. He starved to death intentionally. I did not know until later about my son. If it had not been for one of the other angels we called Gabriel, who watched over all of Eden after I was banned, I would've never known. God never mentioned Cain's name again after sending him to that forsaken place.

I was so heartbroken; I felt forsaken, alone, empty. But regardless, I still walked the earth from time to time, spreading God's teachings to the humans, and it was getting quite dull. So, I decided that I would have a little fun. That is when I started lying with every woman I could, married and unmarried. I influenced the other men to do the same. I was even drinking alcohol and doing drugs, dancing to the music that the humans had created. Shit, I even helped them create some of the music. I was having the time of my fucking life.

Then I said to myself, "it ain't no fun if God's angels can't get none," so I began to corrupt the angels. I influenced some of the angels to come down to earth and travel with me across the globe. We partied our asses off. I was beginning to hate God more and more each day. He took my son away from me. Therefore I would take his human children and his immortal (angels) children away from him. I made sure that a lot of them got a taste of life on earth. They began having sex with the mortals and reproducing, drinking, drugs, and everything else unholy you can think of.

I was gaining more and more power over the mortals and immortals, to the point where everyone was neglecting their duties. They began to pollute the earth. Nature was beginning to die, and disease began to spread rapidly. I was no longer preaching God's word, but instead, I was teaching my own. My word was the complete opposite of God's. I spread the word about having fun, fornication, partying, drugs, alcohol, and everything else you could think of that was unholy. But here was the thing. I didn't demand these things like my father demanded his word to be followed. I gave everyone the option to have one very important thing. That was free will. And because of that, more and more people began to follow me and acknowledge me as God.

I knew that eventually, I would have the power to overthrow God and take heaven for myself. So I continued to corrupt as many of God's children as I could. I became more powerful than I was when God first blessed me with supernatural abilities. This feeling was better than sex. As I gained more followers, God was beginning to lose his powers. He was growing very weak, but there was still a part of me that loved him. He was the one that gave me life, power, and authority.

I was starting to feel bad for what I was doing to him briefly, but then I heard something that would be the last straw for me. One of the other angels told me that God planned to bring new life to the world in another 1,000 years or so, and he will be claimed as the "King, The True Son of God." This new life would spread joy and preach God's words. He would be in God's perfect image and possess supernatural powers. I asked what will be the name of this new life to come. The angel said, "I think this new life will be named "Jesus Christ.""

CHAPTER 2

And Then He Realized His Hands Were Too Small To Box With God

I couldn't believe it. Another child directly from God named Jesus Christ was in God's plan. The only thing I could think about was if this powerful being was in God's plan, what was God going to do with me? I was so angry and so hurt when I got the news about this "Jesus Christ" that I looked at the angel who gave me this terrible news, and I grabbed him by the neck, extended my big beautiful black wings, and flew to heaven in lightning speed to see my father. Once I reached the front gates of heaven, I melted the gates made of gold and walked through my father's mansion with many mansions holding a half-dead angel by the neck angrily. Once I reached his throne room, I saw God sitting high on his throne, looking down at me with his bright gold eyes. Some of his strongest angels surrounded him. I took the angel that I had in my hand and threw him to the ground at the feet of God's angel/guards. God looked at me angrily and sighed hard. Then he stood up tall at his throne and looked down at me and pointed at me.

"HOW DARE YOU, LUCIFER?!

"HOW DARE YOU?! YOU PLAN ON GETTING RID OF ME! FOR A DAMN HALF-HUMAN, HALF GOD! AFTER

EVERYTHING I HAVE DONE FOR YOU! I HAVE LOVED YOU! WORSHIPPED YOU! SERVED YOU! SPREAD YOUR LAWS AND YOUR WORDS TO YOUR LITTLE EARTHLY MORTAL HUMANS THAT YOU LOVE SOOOOO MUCH. THEY WOULDN'T EVEN EXIST IF IT HAD NOT BEEN FOR ME TELLING YOU TO FILL THE EARTH WITH LIFE! ME! JUST ME!"

"My son, I have no idea what has gotten into you, but you need to think about who you are talking to and what you are saying. Because just like I created these earthly mortal humans as you said, I created you too," God said.

"YES, YOU DID CREATE ME. BUT FOR WHAT? TO SUFFER ALONE? TO SERVE YOU? TO COME SECOND TO YOUR HALF-HUMAN SON JESUS CHRIST?!"

God looked down and shook his head. He walked down from his throne and looked me dead into my eyes as I cried and put his hand on my cheek and wiped my tears with his thumb.

"Lucifer, you're my firstborn; I have plans for you, even though you have defied me in more ways than one. You are the reason for mortality in humans, and you are the reason I had to create Grimm, the angel of death. You are the reason for many bad things, but I still love you, and I still plan to give you something that not even your brother Jesus will inherit. But son, you must repent for your self-destruction and the corruption you have caused. Look at all you have done! You have created unholy acts upon the humans and our heavenly angels. You have everyone disobeying my laws along with you. Now, look at you? Storming up to my throne with one of my children, half-dead, lying on the ground, and for what? Because of your envy of another one of my creations that don't even exist yet? It is stupidity Lucifer. So I am begging you, my son. REPENT!!!!"

"Why should I repent? Look at what you've done to me? You took away my Eve and gave her to that idiot Adam, and then you sent my son to a place where you knew he would die. It is not fair, father. It is not fair!

"Son, I taught you, love, and I taught you patience. And if you had considered those two things, you would've known that eventually, I would have created something better for you than Eve. More beautiful, deserving, and worthy. But Eve was not yours to claim; she was Adam's. Just like that Tree of Life was mine and was not to be touched by anyone, but you influenced Eve to persuade Adam against my laws. Everything I did was for a reason, and you could never see that because you were so jealous of these angels and humans that I intentionally created for you to one day rule. With that being said, son, I plan to still give you everything your heart desires. You will rule heaven and all of my creations. You will have someone of your rib to love you and support you in your Godship. You will have a son in your image just like you are in mine. And it will be all meant for you. But as I said before, son. Repent."

I got down on my knees with tears flowing like a river from my face. All I could think about was how I had to dance to my father's music and follow his every command. I had to wait for him to give me his throne, his creations, a woman of my rib. It was all bullshit. I wanted more. I wanted what I wanted. I wanted Eve, I wanted Cain. And honestly, I enjoyed corrupting his creations too much to stop. So, I looked over at this random-ass half-dead angel lying on the ground, and I walked over and picked him up by his beautiful black wings and ripped them off. I let that angel fall to the ground and looked down at him. I incinerated him with my eyes glowing a bright red and turned him into ashes. At that moment, God's soldiers charged at me with their angel blades and spears, and we all fought to the death. They were coming at me from left to right, right to left. Giving it all they had to defeat me, but they did not have the power to do so. I snatched some of their blades in combat and stabbed them in their shoulders, eyes, heads, and chest. I snatched off my robe and used it as a weapon to strangle some of them.

I fought through all of these angels just to get to my father and kill him because of what he had taken from me.

Once I killed God's elite soldiers, I ran up to him while he stood there and stared at all of the havoc I was causing. He opened his gold and black cloth robe and threw his hands in the air. When he did, a bright light appeared from his palms until two angel blades appeared in his hands. His long white dreadlocks turned from white to gold. His robe was glowing, and his eyes.... his eyes had gold lightning coming from them. He no longer looked like a weak, frail immortal. He looked like the God that created me. I looked at him, and I froze and stared at him. Not because I was shocked, but because I was terrified of what he was about to do to me. In a loud, strong deep voice, God said,

"THE BOND HAS BEEN BROKEN! I WILL NO LONGER TOLERATE YOU OR YOUR UNGRATEFUL-NESS! YOU ARE A PAIN! A NUISANCE! A SIN AMONGST SINS. THE GREATEST EVIL TO EVER BE CREATED! AN EMBARRASSMENT! YOU, MY SON, ARE SATAN! A BEAST! A DEVIL! AND NOW I WILL DEFEAT YOU," God growled with his loud, strong, deep voice.

"Well, bring it on, father. Let's see what you're made of with your cute little golden braids and your cute little dull knives! HA!"

All the fear that I had left my body entirely because I knew it was time for me to fight the only being stronger than me. My father. I picked up one of the dead angel's wings that I had killed and turned it into a mighty blade. And then, it was on. I charged after my father and swung my blade at him, and I missed. He dodged by taking a step to the left and elbowed me in my spine. I fell to the ground in pain and agony. But I didn't give up. I got right back up and stood tall on my feet. God laughed at me and said, "Ha, look at you. Made in my image, yet you are so weak. Mentally, emotionally, and physically weak. I guess I thought if I had made you the mirror image of myself, you would be exactly like me. But you're evil. Your envy of the humans and the other angels have consumed your heart, and that makes you weak. I am disappointed."

I looked up at my father and said, "Maybe if you'd just given me what I wanted in the first place, I wouldn't be like this. I don't have access to Eve. My son is dead, and soon, you will be too." Then I charged after my father again while he stood and awaited my attack. He smirked and stepped to his right. I missed him again and fell to the ground. He stood over me, looked down at me, and then stabbed me in my back with one of his blades. I screamed so loudly in pain and agony I hurt my own ears. God then picked me up by my long hair and repeatedly punched me in my face, and then he tossed me across his throne room into a statue made in my likeness. I wanted to just lay down and give up, but I did not stop. I found extra strength and extended my huge black wings, and I charged at God again. This time I grabbed him and flew around with him while repeatedly punching him in various parts of his body. God finally caught my fist, and he extended his wings made of pure gold, swung me around in a circle, and released me to hit the ground. Then He flew down and charged at me with his blade and stabbed me in the stomach. I grabbed him by the throat, but I did not have the strength to choke him. But God, on the other hand, had all of the strength in the world. He grabbed me by my throat, and he then said,

"I watched your son die, and I enjoyed it. I knew he would become evil. Cain was not born out of love and honesty. He was born out of hate, deceit, and jealousy."

"I hate you, father."

"I love you too son."

God lifted me in the air by my throat with one hand and snapped his fingers with his other hand. Out of nowhere, all of the angels that were committing sins against God appeared before me in chains and shackles. Then God pointed to the ground opening a portal, and said, "I hate that this had to happen, but you and those who have sinned against me are no longer welcome here in my mansion that has many mansions." You SHALL BE CAST OUT!" The next thing I knew, God took his other hand and snapped his fingers again. In a single snap, God had sent all of the angels that followed me in my corruption through that portal. At that moment, I was afraid because I did not know where that portal led to when he first opened it. Then God looked me deep into my eyes and dropped me in that portal.

As I fell through that portal, I looked up at my father. My father, God, looked down at me and the portal was beginning to close. I could see him crying, and even felt some of his tears fall on my face and in my mouth. I do not know why but it gave me a burst of strength, and it actually healed the scars from our battle. As I fell from heaven along with the other angels. I passed the stars, the moon, the sun, and all of these other planets that God and I had created. Then next thing I knew, the fallen angels and I entered into earth's atmosphere and hit the ground in different parts of the earth like heavy boulders falling from a cliff. Some of the angels that landed near me were dead. The ones who had survived had no more powers, their wings had shredded off of their backs, and they had no memory of who they were. Me on the other hand, I didn't lose a thing. And to this day, I still don't know why. But I still had every ounce of power I had before attacking God in heaven. I still had my wings. I lost no memory. I was still the most beautiful angel God had ever created and the most powerful. And I knew that this battle was not over. Far from it! It was time for me to take what I wanted!

CHAPTER 3

And Then There Was Hell

Since I was cast away from heaven, I no longer had to follow God's laws. So after thoughtlessly wandering the earth for so many years, still causing corruption. But I had such an empty void in my life. That void was Eve. I wanted to see my beautiful Eve. So I went back to the Garden of Eden, hoping that I would see her. When I arrived I saw a whole civilization, built all across the beautiful land. Children were playing, the young men and women were tending to the garden and the elders sat and shared stories of their past lives. Homes were built, and the people even had a political system in place. It was amazing how Eden had changed so much after all these years. As I walked through Eden I saw a tall man with pure white hair, with a younger woman and small children surrounding him. These younger children called him father. I approached this man because I just knew I was losing my fucking mind. It couldn't be who I thought it was. It was fucking Adam, but there was no Eve. Adam looked at me with disgust and then decided to walk over to me.

"What are you doing here Lucifer? You should not be here, for you have deceived God," Adam said.

"I am no longer following God, I follow my own path, where is Eve?"

He looked at me and smiled and chuckled. "She's dead." I thought he was lying at first. So I grabbed Adam by his neck lifting him off the ground and demanded the truth. Adam then said "She died on her journey to West Eden, to find your son. Why do you think I have a new wife? God has blessed me with a new family, a wife that is very loyal and more children. And although I will not live long enough to see them all grow to be strong adults, at least I can die happy."

I let Adam go and left the Garden of Eden. I traveled long and far to get to West Eden. When I arrived it was dark, and very cold. The land was so dry if you dragged your feet across the sands, you could probably set fire. As I walked further through West Eden, I noticed a dried up dead tree, and something was under it. With the cold air blowing sand in my eyes it was hard to see what it was. When I got closer to the tree, I was heartbroken. I saw these two skeletons lying on the ground. It looked as if one was holding the other. Adam did not lie, Eve was dead, and she was holding our son before she had died. I never really felt pain before, but now I did. I screamed to the top of my lungs, I cried so hard my tears flowed like a river. I was hurt, angry, and heartbroken. I was alone.

West Eden was the center of the earth, and I decided that I would make this part of the earth my own, just as God did with the Tree of Life in the garden. I made sure West Eden was a place where God's Rejects would come. The ones who were turned away from the gates of heaven because they were perfect imperfections like myself. The ones who were forever to walk this earth. These rejects would serve me and be a part of my army. They would feel pain, and they would also inflict it in any way they possibly could. In due time, I had all intentions to charge through heaven's gates with this army. So I changed everything about West Eden in order to house these lost souls, even the name. Instead of West Eden being called West Eden, it would be referred to as HELL. Here Eternally Lives The Lost. I had lost my soul, and others were losing theirs every second I stood in West Eden. In my heart there was nothing but fire in it. And as much as I wanted to set fire to this dry land, I knew that I could not do that. I had to blend in. Hell couldn't be hot, filled with fire like I wanted to be. So I gave it life, I built homes. Put trees, water and plants in this place in a single snap. I had made this land for the living, the dead, and the living dead. Because no matter who you were or what you were, if you were an undesirable in God's eye, you were welcome to come to Hell.

Before I fell from grace, God called me a " satan and the devil" or whatever the fuck. I just told you all earlier, and I don't even remember all the damn names he called me. Now ain't that a bitch? But anyway, I planned to put all of those names to work to show what I was really about. I wanted to give my father hell. Most importantly, I wanted to kill him, take over heaven, and finish corrupting his precious angels and perfect mortal creations and use them against him. Soon, hell would form to be one of the worst parts of civilization the world will ever see, and they will be filled with all of God's REJECTS!

The End... For Now

CHAPTER 4

Outro Song: Many Mansions

Many mansions in his mansion and I was cast out,
Of my father's house, now tell me what the fuck that's bout.
Cause an angel wanted to bring some party to life?
Or is it cause I fucked the first man's wife?
Could be a lot of things,
I've done so many things,
So many evil things,
But were they evil things?
Nothing is what it seems,
Not even my story,
Scriptures paint me in an image that's so evil and gory.
Y'all call me the devil,
Gave me a bad name.
Wanna put me to shame,
That's how I got my fame.
All of you hoes are lame.
Y'all need ya asses whipped,
Let me go to the tree of life and cut me a switch.

Welcome To 10-5 (Hell)
The Devil's Advocate
Check Out This Preview of What Is To Come!

Prelude: Welcome to 10-5 (Hell)

Time. Where did it go? Did it disappear? No. It just passed by. But why? Is it because since the last time you heard from me, my brother was put on the cross to die? Is it because Moses parted the red sea? And during that time, the Pharoah of Egypt rejected his God and embraced me? Is it because slavery of the black race took the world by storm? And the civil war left so many people to mourn? Is it because there have been so many evils in the world since God rejected me? That time has escaped all of our grasps, and the results of all of this evil is what you all have seen and still will see? Time, where did it all go? I don't know. And I don't give a shit. Because now the year is 1936, and peep this. Just like God has his chosen few, I do too.

One of my chosen few was a small child. A baby if we are to be a little more specific. A baby born into a family that God took a liking to. This child's name was Joseph James Williams. Born and raised in Leeds, Alabama, August of 1936. Parents, Willie Joseph Williams Sr and Esther May Williams. Oldest brother, Willie Joseph Williams Jr, (Aka Willie Jr). All three of these people were kind-hearted people. Didn't question a fucking thing that came out of the bible and was obedient to the scripture. These people were poor, didn't have much, but were always able to feed others in need, always helping someone out. And God always made a way for them to get whatever it was that their hearts desired. So I knew that these three could not be touched and that God had a great plan for this family. Their faith was too strong. Since I knew that, I had to corrupt Willie and Esther's second-born child. That's right, Joseph James Williams. Because I had to ruin something that God meant to be good, and any child born into a family like that was destined to come out good. But not Joseph, nooooooooo not him. Because he was my special little project.

When Joseph was a baby, I would wait until everyone in the house was asleep and go into his room and hold him, play with him, and tell him what his destiny truly was. I did this from the moment he was born. I had to get an early start on corrupting him. I would make him fall asleep by walking around the room with him and telling him stories of how hell was built from the moment God cast me from heaven and how it had evolved into a city called Cleveland, Ohio, and how the center of it was a street/neighborhood called East 105th Street. Before I would make this beautiful brown-skinned baby with a head full of hair fall asleep, he would grab my long jet black dreadlocks and beard and giggle and laugh. I enjoyed him so much as a baby. Some might even say that I fell in love with this child as if he was my own. I even made it so that he was the only human that could even see me. As time went by, I continued to do the same thing every night. And then the next thing I knew, Joseph was five years old, and Willie Jr. was fifteen years old.

Joseph and his brother had to go to church with the family every Sunday. Every time they walked into the church, Joseph always asked his parents and his brother the same questions. "Why is Jesus white? Why we don't know what God look like but we know what Jesus look like? How come I don't ever see God, but I see the Devil all the time?" They always ignored him because they were hoping he'd just shut the fuck up. So when he would come home and get ready for bed, I would be right there sitting in his rocking chair waiting for him.

He would climb into his bed and turn his lamp off and look at me and ask me a series of questions every night, especially when they left church. But one night, Joseph and I had a conversation that disturbed me to a certain degree. He had gotten into bed and looked over at me and began to ask questions.

"Lucifer, why doesn't the bible acknowledge Cain as your son?"

"What do you mean Joseph?"

"Well, don't you think that it is unfair that the bible talks about how Adam and Eve had Cain and Abel, but the bible doesn't mention that you're Cain's father?"

I'd never told Joseph about Adam, Eve, Cain, or even Abel! But I refused to show this child how disturbed I was because I was grooming him since he was born to rule hell. It would make me look weak if I were to show him that anything rattled me because then he would not follow in my footsteps. So I responded calmly.

"Well, Joseph, it is a long story, but how do you know that Cain is my son? I never told you that."

"My brother Junior told me. God speaks to him just like you speak to me."

"Have you ever told your brother that you speak to me?"

"No."

"What about your parents?"

"No, I haven't told anyone about you. My parents wouldn't believe me, and my brother would try to turn me against you. But I like you. You're my best friend."

"You're my best friend too. Which is why you are going to be the true ruler of this universe. You just watch."

After that conversation, Joseph went to sleep, and I sat there in Joseph's rocking chair with a bit of fear inside me. At that moment I realized that God was waging a war against me just as I was waging a war against him. But the last time that we went head to head, he defeated me and that is what scared me. If he was speaking to this child, he was grooming him to be his prophet on earth. And a prophet of God's is a dangerous being. So I got out of the chair and walked through the Williams's house and when I got to Willie Jr's room, I had all intentions of killing him. But the second that I touched the doorknob, the door shocked me and shined a bright gold light. That is when I realized that God was protecting him. So there was only one thing that I could do. And that was to create the biggest fucking gangsta the world had ever seen to terrorize everyone. Someone who would not only rule hell, but raise hell, and kill anyone who got in his way. Including his own brother because I was not going to let my father get the upper hand on me! Not again! Not This Time...

(End of Preview)

I hope you all enjoyed this preview of "Welcome to 10-5 (Hell) The Devil's Advocate." To stay updated on future projects and release dates, please scan the qr code below to follow
Iconic Creations Entertainment on Instagram:

Also, please scan the second qr code to follow
Ahmad "Gemini" Ray: